TEAM SPORTS

By Heather Hammonds

Illustrations by Samantha Asri

T0342767

Contents

Join a Team Sport

Participation in a team sport is one of the best ways to have fun and spend time with others.

There are many reasons why joining a team sport can be beneficial.

First, it is important for everyone to do physical exercise to stay fit and healthy. Most team sports are a good way to do this because they involve running, jumping and other physical activities. Physical exercise helps make us stronger.

Second, a large number of exciting games are played as team sports.

Teams can take part in competitions or just play together socially.

Basketball is a popular team sport. Volleyball, soccer, softball, cricket and hockey are too. People can generally join a team at their local sports centre or sports ground. Then they can play against other teams in their area.

Third, team sports are an excellent way to meet new people and make new friends. This is because people playing on the same team are usually about the same age. They often have similar interests.

Fourth, team sports are a good family activity. Several members of one family may play on the same team, or at different levels depending on their age. Parents also help out at their children's competitions or practice sessions.

Fifth, playing a team sport in a competition is very exciting. Team members work together to try to help their team win. They cheer each other on and support each other.

To sum up, playing a team sport is a great way to have fun, make friends and get the exercise we all need. Playing at least one team sport is highly recommended as part of an exercise routine.

We Won!

Yesterday afternoon our class travelled by bus to the Sports Centre. We watched our school basketball team play against the Seaspray School team. It was an extremely exciting match.

I thought the Sports Centre was huge. It had several basketball courts. The floor of the courts was made of polished wood. The courts looked shiny and new.

All the spectators cheered when the teams came onto the court. We cheered the loudest for our school. I noticed some of the players on Seaspray's team looked very tall and strong. Most of our team members were smaller, but they were excellent players. I hoped we could win!

The game began and the players raced speedily around the court with the ball. The game was fast and frantic. Seaspray's team scored the first four goals. Their tallest player scored the fourth goal and the crowd roared.

Then our team got possession of the ball and began to fight back. Our players tried their hardest. The soles of their shoes squeaked on the shiny floor as they bounced the ball and ran.

By half-time, the scores were even. Our school sports coach was obviously pleased with our players because he was smiling as he talked to them.

Our team played well in the third and fourth quarters. They threw the ball expertly to each other and scored lots of goals. By the end of the game, our school had won. I cheered so loudly that I almost lost my voice.

Next year, I am going to join the school basketball team myself!